SAFE AT HOME

Robert Skead, Safe at Home

ISBN 1-887002-91-X

Cross Training Publishing
317 West Second Street
Grand Island, NE 68801
(800) 430-8588

This book is manufactured in the United States of America.

Library of Congress Cataloging in Publication Data in Progress.

Published by Cross Training Publishing,
317 West Second Street
Grand Island, NE 68801
1-800-430-8588
Website: crosstrainingpub.com

"Every day is a new opportunity.
You can build on yesterday's success
or put its failures behind and start over again.
That's the way life is.
With a new game every day.
And that's the way baseball is."

Bob Feller
Indians Pitcher (1936-56)

Contents

CHAPTER ONE
Leading Off

"Fifty thousand dollars!?" exclaimed eleven-year-old Trevor Mitchell. He couldn't believe it. He looked at his dad who was standing there dazed with his mouth wide open.

"That's what the book says," replied Charlie, the owner and proprietor of Charlie's Sports Collectibles. "Dave, come here! Take a look at this," Charlie beckoned with excitement. "This is beautiful! Where did you get this?" Charlie asked Trevor and his father.

Trevor's father was still speechless. Hearing the words fifty thousand dollars sometimes does that to people. "Ummm. Oh, I'm sorry," Trevor's father said, coming out of his trance. "It was my grandfather's. He gave it to my son yesterday."

"Well, I'll be . . . " Dave, the assistant store manager, kicked in. His smile was wide. He looked at the card as if it were a beautiful diamond. "A 1915 rookie Babe Ruth card . . . in mint condition. In all my years of collecting, I've never seen one in person."

"You say it was your grandfather's?" Charlie asked.

"My great-grandfather's," Trevor replied, not knowing that Charlie was addressing his father.

"I thought it might be valuable, but I never imagined . . . " Trevor's dad said. "That's why we're here. I didn't want Trevor to . . . well, you know . . . "

"First things first," Charlie said taking out a sturdy plastic card holder. "Let's make sure this baby stays protected." He slipped the card carefully into the holder with the precision of an expert.

"This is in perfect condition. Where has it been?" Charlie asked.

"My grandfather kept it in a special place in the back of his Bible," Trevor's dad replied.

"Oh," said Charlie, not knowing what else to say. "Mr. . . . ?"

"Mitchell," Trevor's dad filled in.

"Mr. Mitchell, this is a spectacular card. It may even be worth a little more than fifty thousand. This book is six months old."

"Wow," Trevor exclaimed, his eyes growing wider. Being young, he hadn't come to fully appreciate the value of the dollar, but he could tell from everyone's reaction that this card was special. Its prescribed monetary value, however, meant nothing to Trevor. The card held value to him because of the great man who gave it to him–and because of the story behind it.

At this moment, a man who had been browsing through the shop, which contained various sports cards, collectibles and memorabilia, came over to take a look at the card. His name was Mike Tripuka. Charlie knew Mike's profession, but Trevor and his dad had no idea.

"May I?" Mike asked Trevor's father.

"Sure," he replied handing him the card now protected from harm in its new plastic case.

"Wow, Babe Ruth . . . the Sultan of Swat. He was truly a great hitter."

"The greatest," added Dave Simms.

"Not many people know, but the Babe was also a great pitcher," Mike went on to say.

Trevor's eyebrows raised with interest. He wanted to say something badly, but his dad taught him not to interrupt adults while they are speaking.

"Babe Ruth himself said his favorite record is the one he held for 29 2/3 consecutive scoreless innings pitched in World Series play."

A pause. Trevor jumped in. "I know he was a great pitcher!" Trevor proclaimed.

All the men turned their attention to him now, impressed by his statement.

"My great-grandpa told me. My great-grandpa played baseball with Babe Ruth. That's why he has this card."

"How old is your great-grandfather?" Charlie asked.

"A century! Isn't that awesome!" Trevor answered.

"He turned 100 yesterday," Trevor's father replied.

"Well, I'll be," Charlie said shaking his head in wonder. "That is wonderful!"

"Really?" Mike replied with interest. Charlie and Dave looked at Mike. They had an idea what Mike was thinking. You see, Mike Tripuka was the local sportswriter—and like all writers, he was always looking for a story.

"One hundred?" Mike questioned. "And you say he played ball with Babe Ruth? In the Majors?"

"Yep," Trevor said proudly.

His dad knew what was coming next, and he felt a bit awkward because of it.

"And he even stole home while the Babe was pitching. The only person to ever do it."

The store fell silent for a moment as they all took this information in. They didn't know if this was true or just the fabricated story of an imaginative child.

They looked at Trevor's dad who, still feeling awkward because he knew the statement sounded unbelievable, paused for a second, then said, "It's true."

Mike Tripuka had to think fast. *A one-hundred-year-old man who played ball with Babe Ruth. He even stole home while the Babe was pitching. A fifty-thousand-dollar card.* Then his mouth began to move before he even realized it. "May I talk to your grandfather sometime?" he asked Mr. Mitchell. "I'm Mike Tripuka, sportswriter for the *Suburban Times.* I'd really like to meet him."

Trevor's dad hesitated for a moment. He looked into Mike's eyes. He knew the reputation of reporters and how they sometimes distorted the truth. He knew that some even outright lied. So he looked into Mike's eyes, knowing that the eyes reveal the soul.

"Sure," he replied, feeling Mike was trustworthy. "I'll give you our number. He lives with us. Call me, and I'll see what I can do."

Charlie handed Mike a piece of paper. Mike gave the paper to Mr. Mitchell, then pulled out a pen from his blazer. Mr. Mitchell wrote down the number and handed the piece of paper back to Mike.

"Thanks," Mike said, extending his hand.

"No problem," Mr. Mitchell replied as they shook hands.

As he let go of his grip, Mr. Mitchell could not help but wonder if he was doing the right thing. He knew his grandpa's story–and he believed it. However, he wondered if he had just opened up a can of worms that should not have been opened. His own father had passed away three years earlier, so grandpa was still the honorary head of the family. Grandpa was the man who taught his father about what was important in life: God, family, honor, and integrity. His father, in turn, taught him–and he was trying to instill in Trevor those same values. He'd never do anything to intentionally hurt his grandfather.

Should I have given him our number? What would this reporter write? A story about a 100th birthday or a story about a crazy old man who says he stole home off Babe Ruth ? A story he knew left most who heard it in disbelief. What have I done?

"Thanks for the information," Mr. Mitchell said to Charlie and Dave.

Charlie handed the card to Trevor's dad.

"Not me. It belongs to my son."

Charlie handed it to Trevor. "Take good care of that, sport."

"I will," Trevor said.

Trevor's dad reached into his pocket and brought out some money. "How much do I owe for the case?" he asked.

"Nothing," Charlie said. "I should pay you for the privilege of seeing it–and holding it."

"You sure?"

"Hey, you guys made my day today. That card is a thing of beauty," Charlie said.

"Thanks, that's really nice of you," Trevor's dad replied, putting his money away.

"If you ever wanna sell it . . . I can help!" Charlie added.

13

Trevor's father chuckled. "I don't think so. It's kind of a family heirloom. But thanks."

"I'll be in touch!" Mike Tripuka exclaimed, as Trevor and his dad made their way to the door.

"Bye!" yelled Trevor. "Thanks!"

Trevor looked up at his dad and smiled. His dad put his arm around him and opened the door.

The three men behind them looked at each other as if what had just transpired was something magical, but Trevor held the card tightly in his hand and pondered thoughts of his great-grandpa in his heart. For Trevor and his great-grandpa shared a special bond—their love for and admiration of a game called baseball.

Little did Trevor know that the card he held in his hand would change the rest of his life.

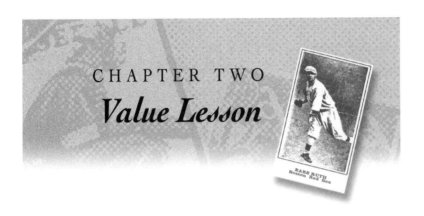

CHAPTER TWO

Value Lesson

"I don't think we should let him keep it," Trevor's dad said, almost whispering.

"Why not?" was the response of Trevor's mom, who was probably the most honest and fair woman around. "Just because it's worth a lot of money?" she added.

"Fifty thousand dollars is more than just a lot of money, dear. Most people don't make that much in a whole year."

"You're stating the obvious," she said. "What do you want to do, sell it?"

"No." A pause. "It's not ours to sell."

"You're right. It's Trevor's."

"I think he's too young to have it. It's worth too much. It's too much responsibility." Another pause. "I'm thinking maybe we should suggest he give it back to grandpa," he said softly, trying not to be heard by ears that didn't need to hear or know everything.

"Grandpa wouldn't take it. He gave it to Trevor for a reason. You know how special Trev is to him."

"I know, but grandpa didn't know how much it was worth," Trevor's dad said.

"He knows now. What did he say this afternoon? . . . He said, 'Fifty grand for a picture of a man on a piece of paper. The Babe is worth more now than when he played.' He then told Trev to 'take good care of it.' Right?"

"That's what I'm talking about. I'm not sure Trevor is old enough to take good care of a fifty-thousand-dollar card."

Trevor stood down the hallway against the wall, listening to his parents' conversation. He couldn't hear every word, but he could hear the important ones. He felt a little guilty listening, being taught not to eavesdrop, but he couldn't just leave now after hearing this much.

Trevor was beginning to understand that maybe there was more to this card than just a special gift from his great-grandpa. It was, after all, just a piece of paper with a picture of the world's greatest baseball player on it. To an adult, however, it had importance because of the monetary value it represented—and when money is involved in any situation, adults tend to start acting differently. Trevor was learning this lesson of life earlier than most—maybe too early.

"It is a big responsibility," his mother replied. "Not many children own something worth that much money, but then again, it is his card. We can't take it away from him."

"We can suggest that we hold it for him though, and that whenever he wants to see it, he's welcome to."

Trevor listened to what his dad had proposed. The card was his, but as he heard his parents talking and listened to their concern, he really didn't care whether they held it or not. He had only owned it for one day.

"That just doesn't feel right," his mother said. "The card

is his. It was a gift to him. I say we let him have responsibility for it. We've been teaching him to give generously and be responsible with his money, why should this be any different? I say we explain to him the value it represents, even though there are only a handful of people who'd actually pay that much for it, and let him enjoy it."

"You're right," Trevor's dad said. "It's a big one—but we'll give him ultimate responsibility for it. Bottom line is, we can't take it away from him." A pause. "We'll make one rule—the card doesn't leave this house."

All that having been said, Trevor's mom put her arms around her husband and gave him a kiss.

"Good idea. I love when you agree with me, " she said kiddingly, while looking him in the eyes.

"I bet you do," he joked back.

"Hey, Solomon was just a boy when he was king, and he had responsibility for a whole nation."

"Yeah, but he was also the wisest person to ever live," Mr. Mitchell added.

Trevor's mom kissed her husband again.

Trevor could hear the smooching from down the hall. *Oh, man, do they have to do that?* he thought, and he retreated to his room knowing the card would be his responsibility.

He picked up the card from his dresser and looked at "The Babe." The photograph depicted him in pitching motion. He thought about his great-grandpa standing in the batter's box watching "The Babe's" wind up—and Babe jumping up as great-grandpa drilled one right between his legs. He laughed out loud to himself.

Then he thought about the card's fifty-thousand-dollar value. *Fifty thousand dollars? That's gotta be a lot of money.*

CHAPTER THREE
The Connection

Mike Tripuka waited for what he felt was an appropriate amount of time to place his call—a polite 24 hours. He'd thought about Trevor and his dad, the card and their story, and he couldn't wait to meet a 100-year-old man who played ball with George Herman "Babe" Ruth.

The phone rang. Trevor's sister, Kirsten, fielded the call and quickly delivered the phone to her father. It was Sunday afternoon, and the Mitchell family had just returned from church where the morning's praise and worship rejuvenated the entire family.

In the back of his mind, Trevor's dad was hoping that this call would not come. He never expected that his grandfather turning 100 two days ago would bring about this kind of attention. He answered the call politely, knowing what Mike wanted. He then put Mike on hold while he asked his grandfather how he would feel about talking to a local reporter about turning 100 and about playing against Babe Ruth many, many years ago.

Trevor's great-grandpa was not the kind of man who would turn down the opportunity to tell his favorite story. Trevor's dad knew this, but had to ask anyway and within an hour, Mike Tripuka was sitting on the front porch drinking lemonade and listening to grandpa tell his amazing story. Trevor and his father were there, too, listening—and enjoying every word, though they had heard it many times before. Stories never seem to get old when they are told with charisma and passion, two qualities which Trevor's great-grandfather, Jack Mitchell, possessed in great quantities.

"The year was 1915," Jack Mitchell started. "It was my rookie year and the first time I ever faced Babe Ruth, who was a rookie the year before. Now, Babe Ruth was a cocky son of a gun. His team, the Red Sox, were good, and he thought that he was the greatest thing to happen to the game since the invention of the ball, which ended up being true. He was great. Everyone knows that. But did you know that there is only one person in the world who ever stole home on him?" Jack Mitchell loved setting up his story.

"It's true," he said as Trevor, his father and Mike Tripuka smiled. "And you're looking at him."

At this point, no one who has ever heard the story knows whether to believe him or not. The fact of the matter is, Trevor's great-grandpa never lies. And if they kept records then like they do today, you could look it up.

"You see, Babe Ruth, for as great as he was, was loud and obnoxious," he said. "I hated that about him. So I made up my mind that when I heard this guy chatter, I was gonna do something about it. I didn't know what at the time, but I knew I was going to do something. This thought occurred to me as I stood in the on-deck circle waiting for my turn at bat.

"Now, our team was really razzing 'The Babe.' And he had no trouble razzing us back. He used words that were making grown men blush. I knew right away this wasn't Sunday School. His reputation had preceded him, and I felt like David against Goliath. So, when it came my turn to bat, I said a little prayer.

"Now, back in those days I wasn't much of a prayin' man, but I said, 'Lord, this guy is full of pride. Help me put him in his place. If you ever answer one of my prayers, please . . . do it now.' " Jack Mitchell paused reflectively. "And what happened after that prayer was a series of wonderful, God-given events."

Mike Tripuka looked at Jack Mitchell with extreme curiosity. He'd never heard anything like this before in his life.

"The Babe got two quick strikes on me, as I swung and missed two perfectly placed pitches. He then missed with two balls and a third which almost knocked me on my derriere.

"With a full count, I prayed again . . . 'Lord, please?'

"The Babe let the ball go, it came speeding toward me and bam! I hit that sucker right up the middle–right between Babe Ruth's legs. He had to jump to not get hit you know where. And there I was–standing on first base."

"Nice job!" Mike exclaimed, laughing and smiling from ear to ear.

"But God's blessings didn't end there," Jack Mitchell went on.

"Now, the men in our dugout were really gettin' on Babe's case, which didn't make him happy.

"I took a good lead off first and Babe immediately let me know he was in charge with a very quick pick off move. And he caught me. Silence fell across the stadium. I raced toward second as the first baseman ran me down. He threw the ball to the shortstop waiting at second, and I was caught in a pickle. The shortstop ran at me, threw the ball back to Babe at first. I took off again toward second, and the Babe ran after me.

"The Good Lord as my witness, what happened then can only be seen as a miracle. I was running hard and fast and my cap flew off, as caps do, moments after the Babe had thrown the ball to second to get me out. As the ball left Babe's hands heading toward second, it miraculously collided with and landed in my cap as it flew in the air behind me. And there I stood safe at second."

Mike Tripuka's mouth was wide open. Trevor's father looked at Mike and didn't know what to think. Trevor listened intently, hanging on every word.

"Babe Ruth looked me square in the eye with a look that said, 'You lucky duck,' although he probably wouldn't have phrased it that way.

"Babe proceeded to strike out the next batter with ease. Then, something divine happened again. As the catcher was throwing the ball back to Ruth, I heard a voice. It said one word—softly, but clearly . . . 'Run!'

"I hesitated a fraction of a second, then I took off toward third.

"Shocked, the Babe must've seen me out of the corner of his eye, and he threw the ball as fast as he got it to Mike McNally at third. I slid and the ump pronounced me 'Safe!'"

At this point, everyone who had ever heard this story begins to think that Trevor's great-grandpa was totally off his rocker. From the expression on Mike Tripuka's face, he may have been thinking the same thing. Keep in mind, however, that truth is sometimes stranger than fiction. And Trevor's great-grandpa spoke the truth–and he always gave credit where credit was due.

"It just goes to show there is power in prayer," he'd say.

"What happened after that is what I told you 'bout earlier–and the reason good ol' Babe Ruth, the Sultan of Swat, the Bambino himself, never forgot my name," he said.

"There I was, standing on third. The men on my team were looking at me as if I were something they had never seen before and praising me before 'The Babe.' I didn't even have time to revel in the moment, and I heard it again. 'Run.' I didn't believe it, and I stood still as the Babe threw a strike.

" 'Lord,' I said. 'You can't be serious.' I didn't hear Him speak again, but a Scripture came to my mind. Something I heard years before in Sunday School. It was 'Does God speaketh and then not act.' I knew I had to do something.

"As the Babe began his wind-up, I decided to trust the Lord. I ran. I took off as fast as I could and ran as straight and as hard as I could with my eyes fixed on one goal– home plate.

"There wasn't time for me to signal the batter. Fortunately, he saw me coming and knew not to swing.

"The 90 feet seemed to take forever, each step of the way my heart beating faster and faster. I saw the goal and began my slide.

"I touched the plate milliseconds before I was tagged by the catcher and the ump yelled 'Saaaaafe!!!' The crowd went wild, and so did our bench.

"You should have seen the look on Babe Ruth's face. He looked at me like I had ten legs and three heads. He was definitely humbled. I wish someone had a picture of it to show you, but I have it right up here," he said, pointing to his forehead.

"Never before and never since has anyone stolen home off of Babe Ruth. God was surely with me that day, and He's been with me ever since. Actually, He's been with me since the day I was created in my mother's womb. Isn't it wonderful? God is so faithful," he said beaming. "And that's when I discovered that He really does answer prayer."

Trevor's great-grandpa loved to tell that story. Every time he told it he sounded like a boy again.

Mike paused for a long moment soaking it all in. "Wow, that is some story!" Mike exclaimed. "You remember everything?"

"Like it was yesterday," Trevor's great-grandpa replied. "Like it was yesterday."

Mike sipped his lemonade and exchanged a subtle look with Trevor's dad. Mike seemed to search for some clue in his eyes—was this for real?

Trevor's dad felt at that moment that he never should have let this meeting happen. He only hoped he was right in his initial judgement of the man sipping lemonade before him.

"Wow," Mike said politely. "And you held onto the card all these years?"

"Yes. A good friend gave it to me shortly after it happened, and I held onto it."

"And now your great-grandson has it?"

"That's right."

Mike jotted some notes down on his pad, but with a

story like this, notes were really not necessary. If anything was memorable, this certainly was.

"Who may I ask is your favorite baseball player?" Mike inquired. He was a sports reporter after all, and sports was his first love.

Jack Mitchell did not hesitate. "Christy Mathewson," he said.

"Now there was a great pitcher," Mike added. "Many believe he is the greatest pitcher of all time. They say he could hit a tin cup from pitching distance. Talk about control."

"Another great thing about Christy Mathewson was that he was a man of strong conviction. Before he entered the big leagues, he promised his mom that he would never pitch a game on Sunday. They called him 'The Christian Gentleman.' Even the reporters loved him . . . And reporters could use their pen to make or break you." Trevor's great-grandpa suddenly remembered who he was talking to. "Sorry," he said.

"No offense taken," Mike affirmed. A pause. "Mr. Mitchell, what do you think is the secret to a long life?"

Jack Mitchell hesitated for a moment, then chuckled. "Well, at my age I've got one foot in the grave and another on a banana peel."

Trevor's dad rolled his eyes. It was a line he's heard his grandpa say at least a thousand times.

"But, seriously, " Jack went on, "there's no secret really. It's a gift. I've done nothing to deserve living this long. With all the things I've done wrong in my life, it's a wonder I'm still here at all. Every day is a gift, a gift from God . . . whether you're 11, 50 or 100."

Mike was now writing fast on his pad, wishing he had

tape-recorded the entire conversation. He had prepared a few other questions to ask, but somehow they seemed inappropriate now. He folded his notebook and tucked his pen inside its spiral binding.

"Thank you so much Mr. Mitchell, Mr. Mitchell" and he looked at Trevor, "and Mr. Mitchell . . . for your time. This is an incredible story." He turned his attention to Trevor. "Think you'll ever sell that card, kid?"

"No way," Trevor proclaimed.

"I didn't think so. Thanks, everyone!" Mike was like a kid who just received a new toy and couldn't wait to go home and play with it.

And with that, the interview was over, and Mike Tripuka was gone.

Trevor's dad still couldn't help but wonder what the future held–and if he did the right thing letting this happen.

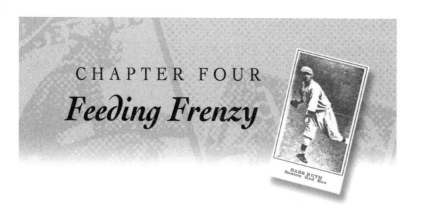

CHAPTER FOUR
Feeding Frenzy

The piece was cleverly titled "The Oldest Old-Timer," and appeared in the human interest section of the *Suburban Times,* a section Mike Tripuka had never appeared in before. His forte was sports, but because of the age of the person featured in this story, his editor thought this piece would best serve his publication's audience by appearing as "human interest."

Mike Tripuka did what every good reporter does—he went home after the interview and started his research. His first job was to see if there were any records of the game. He checked his *Baseball Encyclopedia* and numerous other books of baseball statistics and records. There were plenty of records that stated Jack Mitchell played in the Major Leagues, but as for the game in question, he found nothing.

He then went on the Internet to see if any information on the game in question existed on the world wide web. There was nothing.

His last effort (*which should have been my first,* he thought) was to call Cooperstown and speak to the librarian at the Baseball Hall of Fame. The story Mike told sounded familiar to the librarian, but there were lots of stories and fables about baseball's golden age—and this was just one of a thousand that were out there.

The librarian called Mike back one hour later with news that there were no records about that game in the Hall of Fame Library, "but . . ." he went on to say, "it doesn't mean that the game never happened." It seems that there were about four games in baseball history, from about 1911 to 1932, that no one, not even the Hall of Fame, had records of. No one knows if these records were stolen, lost or still in the basement in some forgotten section of the "Hall" or sports publication.

As a matter of fact, many years earlier, a good friend suggested to Trevor's great-grandfather that maybe "The Babe" himself arranged to have the records of the game "misplaced" so that the game and what happened would be "erased" from existence, at least on paper anyway.

Great, Mike thought to himself. *This changes everything.*

Trevor's dad wasn't the first person in the family to read the story. That honor went to Trevor's mom who was home when the paper arrived. She immediately called her husband and gave him the news.

Trevor's father rushed home from work. He owned and ran the local food market, so leaving at the drop of a hat, or sound of a bell in this case, was no big deal.

It would be an understatement to say that Trevor's dad was concerned as he read the article, no matter what his wife told him. *What's the underlying message?* he thought.

He read the article intensely. What he read was simply

the story of a 100-year-old family man who got a hit off of and stole home off of Babe Ruth and a fifty-thousand-dollar card that was a gift to the Old-Timer's great-grandson. Mike left in the part about the ball colliding with the hat, that gave the piece a comic and magical tone. But he strategically left out all the references to Jack Mitchell's prayer and to hearing the voice of God and to the miraculous events of the day.

The story actually made Jack Mitchell sound like a great baseball player. The fact that the story could not be verified by records was also mentioned toward the end, which could leave the reader with the impression that Trevor's great-grandfather made it all up. The impact and truth of the story, like most, was determined by the state of mind of the reader. That part Trevor's dad did not really like.

It could've been worse I guess, Trevor's dad thought to himself.

It could have been just that, but the can of worms was already open—and sometimes things have a way of rapidly getting worse before you even realized a worm was out of the can.

Trevor's great-grandfather, on the other hand, was a little upset that Mike Tripuka didn't include the whole story. He'd dealt with sports reporters during his career, so he wasn't too surprised, but he had hoped for more.

The article appeared in the *Suburban Times* as scheduled. It received great praise from Mike's readers and numerous OpEd letters to the paper on the joys of having "old people" around and how much wisdom and wit they have to share. It was then picked up by the Associated

Press and printed in thousands of newspapers around the country. CNN® even did a five-minute segment on the story with an interview with great-grandpa and Trevor that appeared all over the world. The phone in the Mitchell house practically rang off the hook for days. Everyone was talking about it, even Trevor's classmates.

Unfortunately, the aftermath of this article was going to prove to be a time of trial and testing for the entire Mitchell family, especially Trevor.

CHAPTER FIVE
Truth and Consequences

"He's a liar! Your grandpa lies like a rug!" It was Frank Carbone. Frank was the biggest kid in school. A little on the chunky side, too, but he was known for being the best player in every sport and a savant when it came to sports statistics and trivia.

"Yeah!" a few other boys agreed.

"He is not, I tell ya! And he's my great-grandfather . . . jerk!" That, of course, was Trevor, defending his great-grandpa with every ounce of gusto he had. "My great-grandpa would never lie! Unlike some people 'round here."

The small crowd watching fell silent as Frank Carbone's eyes grew wider. "You calling me a liar?" Frank said, gritting his teeth and leaning close to Trevor's face.

"Everyone in school knows you lie. No one believes what you say. You lied to Mrs. Sikkema last week when she caught you late for class. You're the liar." Trevor's passion for his great-grandpa and the truth was clouding his better judgement. His words were provoking the much larger and stronger Frank to physical action. Trevor knew the power of words, too. He had been taught this lesson by his father. He realized he went too far when he saw the fierce look of anger in Frank's eye. *Uh oh*, he thought. *The eyes do reveal the soul.*

At this point, all eyes on the playground were fixed on Trevor and Frank.

"We're not talking 'bout me, Mitchell. There's no way your great-grandpa stole home off of Babe Ruth. There's not a record to prove it, even the stupid article said that. He probably never even played against him. No records mean there's no proof. I say he's a liar." He leaned in closer. "What are you going to do about it?!"

"He's not a liar," Trevor said through his teeth. He was starting to get angry now, too, and he didn't like the feeling.

Everyone was waiting for the next offensive word to come out and for a fight to start. The playground hadn't seen a fight in two weeks, since Robbie Jones teased Scott Leach about kissing Donna Abbott.

Trevor stood there for a moment contemplating his next move when he remembered something his father had said to him about loving your enemies. He remembered something else, too, a story he heard weeks earlier about how we are supposed to turn our cheek when we are struck, and go the extra mile. He didn't really understand the "extra mile" part, but he understood the meaning of the story. Physical blows were not occurring yet, but they were striking one another with words. This all went through his mind in a flash as his peers stood there waiting. Then it occurred to him.

"I'll prove it to you!" Trevor said with authority.

"Yeah, right," Frank replied.

Trevor bent down and picked up his backpack. He opened the front pocket and slowly pulled out the Babe Ruth card.

"Here . . . if it never happened . . . then why would he have this?"

A series of "Wows" and gasps of air were heard as Trevor held the card for all eyes to see. They heard about its existence—and what it was worth—and they couldn't believe he actually had it and that he brought it to school.

There wasn't a boy in the crowd that day who wouldn't give or trade everything he owned—even their teeth—for that card.

Frank Carbone didn't know what to say at first. Even he was mesmerized by the card's beauty. Then he snapped out of it.

"Old people keep everything. He had it 'cause it was Babe Ruth. What kind of jerk wouldn't keep a Babe Ruth card?"

His reasoning sounded logical to everyone, except Trevor.

"You can think what you like," Trevor said confidently, securing the card in his backpack, "but I'm telling you, my great-grandfather is not a liar. He really did steal home off of Babe Ruth. If you want . . . you can ask him yourself. I'm sure he'd love to tell you all about it."

"That's all right. I don't need to hear more lies. I read about enough already!" Carbone replied, cocky as ever.

"Good morning, everyone!" It was Mr. Jenkins, the principal.

Trevor's teeth were grinding from Frank's comment. He then uttered one word, soft enough for only one person to hear, "Idiot."

Frank Carbone's head whipped around, and he glared at Trevor. Carbone saw the principal coming and casually backed away from Trevor a bit.

"Good morning, everyone!" Mr. Jenkins exclaimed, now in their midst. "Everyone doing all right?"

"Yes Mr. Jenkins, sir. Everything's . . . great," Frank said confidently.

"The bell should ring any second. Get ready for a great day, everyone!"

The small crowd began to disperse. Frank Carbone leaned in toward Trevor. "After school . . . you're dead meat," he said and he walked away, followed by four of his pals.

Slowly, everyone watching began to disperse and go back to their games, conversations, showing off and flirting.

Great, Trevor thought to himself. *What else could go wrong today?*

Trevor felt a friendly slap on the back. "Cool card, man. Good job." It was Scott Whiteman whom the kids all called "Whitey." Whitey was what Trevor's mom described as a "fair-weather" friend. He only called or hung out with Trevor when there was nothing else to do.

"Thanks," Trevor replied.

"Don't sweat Carbone. He's so dumb he could trip over a cordless phone. I heard he once tried to put M&M®'s in alphabetical order," Whitey joked, laughing as he said it.

His comment caused Trevor to smile for a second. But before Trevor could say another word, Whitey had already seen some other friends and was off trying to catch up to them.

Trevor stood there alone thinking how easy it would have been to insult Frank Carbone more or even to fight with him. Defending his great-grandfather's honor was certainly something worth fighting for. But he knew deep inside that it would have been wrong. This was not the time to fight. His father had been teaching him about faith, honor and about loving others. These were more than just words to the members of the Mitchell family. They were actions. They were the foundations on which they lived their lives. His great-grandpa was surely an example of that. And as hard as doing the right thing was, he knew that he was all the better for it. But now, even after having resisted the temptation to fight, he was warned and threatened that a fight would occur after school. *I don't want to fight. How did this happen? What am I gonna do?*

The bell rang. Everyone hustled inside.

Trevor adjusted his backpack around his shoulder and walked inside. The thoughts of a dreaded afternoon fight now encompassed him, and even worse, the words Frank Carbone and the others said about his great-grandfather were now planted in his head—and beginning to take root.

The walk home from school that day was excruciatingly long for Trevor. He could have walked with some other boys and girls, but he chose to walk alone. He could even have walked home a different way to avoid the fight, but the fight wasn't the first thing on his mind, his great-grandfather was. He replayed great-grandpa's story over and over inside his head. It was easy to do, he had heard the story enough times. *It does sound pretty incredible. Maybe they're right. Maybe he did make it up. It's true . . . there are no records to prove it. No records . . .*

It was the first time in Trevor's life the thought ever occurred to him. It was the first time he ever doubted his great-grandfather's word, and it left an uneasy feeling in his stomach.

Trevor turned the corner and began to walk down Butternut Avenue. He was two blocks from home now, and Frank Carbone was nowhere in sight. There were some kids walking about fifty feet behind him and some more on the other side of the street. Trevor could hear them laughing, and he felt as if they were all laughing at him.

He looked to his right and noticed a neighbor, Mrs. Younger, with some groceries. Mrs. Younger was about 65 years old. She had silver hair, and she didn't get around too easily. She had bad arthritis, although she still drove her car. She drove slowly, like many older people, and Trevor heard his dad comment once or twice that it was about time Mrs. Younger gave up her driver's license. She was at her front door, trying to get her key in, while holding a bag of groceries. *I wouldn't try that if I were you.* Crash!

Trevor was right. Before the key was halfway in the lock, the groceries were on the ground. Mrs. Younger lost her balance trying to catch her groceries and fell on the porch. Instinctively, Trevor dropped his backpack inside her front fence and ran to her aid.

"You all right?" Trevor asked, as Mrs. Younger tried to get herself up.

"Yes . . . I'm fine. I hate all these keys. My fingers aren't as nimble as they used to be. Seems like only yesterday we didn't need to lock our front doors."

Trevor bent down and helped her pick up her groceries. He picked up a dented can of prune juice, a box of Entenmanns Chocolate Chip cookies, and a bottle of Gatorade®—the orange kind.

"Here," he said, putting the Gatorade® into the bag.

The Gatorade® was for her twenty-five year old son

Marshal who recently moved back in with her. Trevor had seen him cutting her lawn a few times.

"Thank you so much," Mrs. Younger said gratefully. "Hey . . . I read the article on your grandfather . . ."

"Great-grandfather," Trevor said in a corrective tone.

"He's got quite an imagination," she said. "Good story though."

Trevor didn't want to get into it with her.

"Thanks," he replied. "Need anything else?"

"No . . . I'm all right now," she said. "Here, let me give you something for helping me," she added, reaching into her wallet and pulling out a ten dollar bill.

Trevor saw the ten bucks and was tempted to take it.

"No, you keep it," he said, knowing he shouldn't take money for helping someone and that it was too much for what he had done.

"Come on . . . take it," she insisted.

But Trevor stuck to his guns and started walking down her front stairs.

"Thanks! But you keep it!" he yelled.

Trevor looked up at Marshal Younger walking up the walkway. He had Trevor's backpack in his hand and handed it to Trevor as he walked by. Marshal wore his hair a little past his ear lobes, and he had glasses.

"Here you go, sport," he said, as Trevor received the backpack in his chest.

"Thanks," Trevor replied.

"Caught that story on your grandpa . . . that guy is some character," he said, with a tone of voice that made Trevor feel he didn't believe the story either.

Trevor just smiled and continued on his way. *Doesn't anybody believe it?*

He walked about fifty feet and there in the distance on

the same side of the street was Frank Carbone and three of his pals. *Oh, no.* Trevor began to feel a bit afraid. He casually looked around and behind him. There were still kids walking home from school, but no adults were around. *Lord, help me.* He kept walking.

As a matter of fact, that quickly became his plan—to just keep walking, casually, as if this were any other day and he was walking by any other person. He adjusted his backpack and kept a steady pace. He even began to whistle.

Frank Carbone and his friends, Jim and Tom, saw Trevor coming. They smiled at each other awaiting their prey. As Trevor got closer and closer they were stunned to see him looking calm and whistling. They looked at one another as if they couldn't believe their eyes. *Doesn't he know why we're here?*

Trevor was right in front of them now. He nodded his head and acknowledged them and walked right on by. He kept on walking and whistling, until . . .

"Hey! Butthead!" It was Frank Carbone all right.

Do I stop or keep walking?

"Hey! Loser with the lying grandfather!"

Trevor stopped. *Great-grandfather. Can't anyone get that right?* He then slowly turned around.

"What?" Trevor asked, matter-of-factly.

"What do you mean what? You heard me this morning. I said you were gonna be dead meat, and I meant it."

Trevor had to think fast, again. "Why?"

"Huh?" Frank said confused.

"Why do you want to fight me?" Trevor added.

"Mitchell. Are you forgetting something? You called me an idiot, remember? I don't let anyone call me an idiot. Got it?" He was walking closer to Trevor.

"Listen, Frank, you can hit me if you want, but you know what I'm gonna do?"

"Cry . . . probably," he said laughing. The other boys were laughing, too.

A small crowd of other kids who were walking home stopped and gathered around now, one of which was Trevor's friend Ginger.

"Why don't you leave him alone, Frank?!" Ginger said. "You're such a bully. You think you're so cool."

"You gonna fight his battles?" A pause. "He needs a girl to fight his battles!" Frank said loudly to his audience. With that said, he pushed Trevor hard. Trevor stumbled backwards. His backpack fell off his shoulder and into his hand by his side. "You want her to fight for ya . . . baby?" Frank said provokingly. He pushed Trevor again. This time so hard that Trevor fell down, causing him to release the backpack. It landed by Jim's and Tom's feet.

"Leave him alone, Frank!" Ginger yelled. "Don't you think you're a little bigger than he is? Maybe it's unfair. Or is that too much for your little brain?"

"Hey!" Trevor shouted. He was standing up now, dusting his pants off. "Don't you wanna know what I'm gonna do if you hit me?"

Everyone was shocked, especially Frank and his friends.

"Yeah . . . what?" Carbone asked in his toughest voice.

Trevor waited a moment. Everyone was looking at him.

"Nothing," he said. "I'm gonna do nothing. You can hit me and hit me again, and you know what? I'm still gonna do nothing. Not because I'm afraid," he went on, "but because I don't wanna fight."

Frank looked at him strangely. He never heard anything like this before. Neither had anyone else. Trevor had no idea where his words were coming from.

"If my calling you an idiot made you so mad, then I'm sorry. So go ahead . . . beat me up. Come on . . . get it over with. We all have things to do."

Frank froze. He had no idea what to do. All eyes were on him awaiting his next move. He moved closer towards Trevor. "All right Mitchell. I'll teach you for calling me a jerk . . ." He clenched his fist, pulled back his hand and threw a punch at Trevor. He then pulled his punch, stopping just before his fist connected with Trevor's face. Frank laughed as Trevor flinched.

"Hah!" Frank yelled. "What a loser! I still say your grandfather's a liar. I have two words for you . . . no records." He laughed again, causing his friends to laugh, too. "You're both whackos, I say!" He turned to his friends. "Come on. Let this baby go home to his mother and grandfather!"

Jim was holding Trevor's backpack. He passed it to Tom who shoved it into Trevor's chest. "Here. Have a nice day, Mitchell," Tom said.

With that, the boys all left, and everyone else went on their way back home–except Ginger.

"What a jerk," Ginger commented. "I can't believe that guy." A pause. "You all right?"

"Yeah," Trevor said, tucking his shirt in and adjusting his backpack firmly onto his shoulder. "I'm all right." He smiled. "Thanks for sticking up for me. You realize you almost made things worse, don't you?"

"I would've kicked his butt," Ginger said jokingly holding her hand up for a high five.

Trevor laughed and hit her hand high. "It's a big enough target," he joked. Ginger laughed.

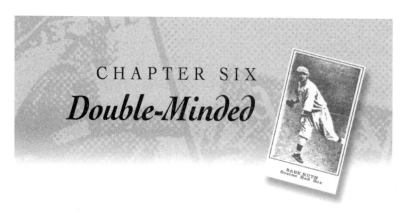

CHAPTER SIX
Double-Minded

No records . . .What if it never really happened? What if he did make it all up? Now that his troubles with Frank Carbone were behind him, Trevor's thoughts were back to his great-grandpa. His eyes were glazed over. He didn't even see or hear the neighbor's dog barking at him as he walked slowly by on the way to his house.

Trevor came through his front door, took off his backpack and put it in its usual spot on the stairs.

He walked inside quietly. He didn't want to talk to his great-grandpa right now. He had too many questions going through his mind. *Please, let him be taking a nap,* he thought.

He saw great-grandpa sitting in his chair. His eyes were closed. *Yes! He's asleep.* Trevor looked again carefully to make sure that great-grandpa was indeed breathing. This was not an unusual experience for Trevor. Sometimes, when he entered a room where great-grandpa was napping, he would immediately start to watch him, staring at his chest to make sure air was coming in and going out.

Trevor watched him for a moment, waiting for his

chest to fill in and out with air. *Good. Still breathing.* Trevor was relieved.

He then looked at his great-grandpa differently. *Why would you make it up? You wouldn't lie to me, would you? to everyone? Why?*

He studied his great-grandpa more, looking at his thick snow white hair, not knowing how a full head of hair is so rare at age 100. He noticed the large brown spots on his great-grandpa's hands. Trevor's great-grandpa was in unbelievably good shape for a man who just turned 100 years old. There are men 25 years old who don't have great-grandpa's love for life. And there are men 70 and above who do not have great-grandpa's physical and mental strengths. Except for eye glasses and an undetectable hearing aid, great-grandpa was in perfect health. He was a man who has been blessed with long life and good health.

On his lap was his Bible. Great-grandpa called it "The Sword of the Lord" because the Word was part of a Christian's armor. Great-grandpa's Bible was practically falling apart, not because it was old, which it was. There are plenty of old Bibles in the world that look brand new. Great-grandpa's Bible looked old because it was well-used. "You can always tell if a man has his act together by whether or not his Bible is falling apart," is what he used to say.

Trevor hated how he was feeling. He always believed anything and everything his great-grandpa told him. *Could this man be a liar? I need to talk to someone . . . but who?*

His friends at school all believed Frank Carbone. Trevor's sister, Kirsten, was older and too wrapped up in her own life and friends to really care how he felt. His best friend in the neighborhood was Ginger, but she hated sports in general, especially baseball. She didn't even have any grandparents that were still living. *She'd never understand.* His father was at work. *I don't want him to know I'm even thinking this way.*

That left one person in Trevor's world to talk to—mom.

"The kids at school are calling him a liar. No one believes it's true. No one believed it happened . . . " Trevor said.

"You know kids your age love to pick on each other; we've talked about that, honey. Don't let it bother you. That's exactly what they want. The more they see that their teasing upsets you, the more they're gonna do it." A pause. "That's one thing your father and I never wanted you or your sister to do is tease another child. Far as we know, you've both been pretty good about resisting that temptation."

"I have, mom," Trevor assured her. "But . . . "

"But what?" she said, with a warm smile.

"But what if they're right? What if he made it all up?"

Trevor's question was sincere; he needed to ask it. He needed to know from someone older—someone with more wisdom about it.

"I mean, there are no records to prove it," Trevor professed. "Even the article said that. Maybe great-grandpa made it all up."

Trevor noticed his mom look over his shoulder. He turned his head and looked into the eyes of his great-grandpa. What he saw is something he'd never forget. Great-grandpa's mouth was turned down.

"Ummm. I was just wondering where you put my glasses?" Jack Mitchell asked.

"They're on the table next to your chair," Trevor's mom answered.

Great-grandpa slowly looked down and shook his head. He didn't say another word. He then looked back up at Trevor and walked away.

Trevor quickly looked back at his mom. She took a deep breath, not knowing exactly what to say.

He looked at his mom. I'm sorry. What do I do? his eyes asked.

She sighed, not having an immediate answer. She knew Jack Mitchell well. Well enough to know that he was very hurt.

"This has got to be the worst day of my life," Trevor said.

"Things are not always easy, are they?" she said, not knowing the half of it.

"Tell me about it," Trevor replied. And he got up off her bed and walked out of the room.

There was only one thing on Trevor's mind now–the card. He wanted to see it. He wanted to believe. So he headed for the stairs and picked up his backpack. Trevor then looked outside and noticed his great-grandfather sitting on the stoop. Great-grandpa's head was down and his eyes were watery. But Trevor didn't know what to say or what to do, so he quietly made his way up the stairs toward his room.

Trevor sat down on his bed, quickly unzipped the front pocket of his backpack and reached inside with tremendous anticipation and . . . it was gone!

CHAPTER SEVEN
Rewind

Panic! *Where is it? I don't believe this!* He turned the pack upside down and dumped its contents onto the bed, shaking the pack, almost violently, making sure nothing could stay inside.

He couldn't scream or yell, although he wanted to. Nobody could know what was happening. *Where is it?! Think. Think. When was the last time I had it? School. I should've never brought it to school. I should've just . . . I had it last at the end of school. I was at my desk putting my books in . . . and it was still there. Then it should be here!*

He ruffled through the bag's contents on his bed. He opened every book, moved every item. All he saw were three spiral notebooks, a math book, pens, pencils, erasers, a pack of Big League Chew®, some empty zip-lock bags and a Granola bar left over from lunch.

Maybe it fell out? He wanted to scream. He checked the zipper on his backpack to see if it was broken. It worked fine.

I should've never taken it out of the house! I lost it!

He knew his parents were forgiving people. Then he remembered his dad really didn't want him to have it. It was worth a ton of money, and they trusted him with it. *Great-grandpa had it for practically eighty years, and I lost it in a week.* He didn't even want to think how his great-grandpa would react. The card was a family heirloom and entrusted to him.

I'm in big trouble. I've gotta find it!

He then remembered that three other people had their hands on his backpack. *Maybe it was stolen. Marshal had it. So did Jim Evans and Tom Murphy. Maybe they took it. But why? They wouldn't . . . they couldn't . . . be that mean? Then again, maybe it fell out. I should look before I go about accusing anyone. Surely, they couldn't have taken it. Oh man!*

Trevor put on his baseball cap, looked down at the floor and backtracked his every step–every place that he and that backpack had been.

He checked the hallway, the stairway. Nothing.

"Bye, mom! I'm going out!" he yelled, his voice cracking. He was out the door in a flash.

He looked everywhere. The walkway, the sidewalk–all along his route home from school and its surrounding areas–anywhere and everywhere the card could have fallen, he looked.

He was thankful he didn't have to worry about the card blowing away. Its heavy plastic protective case would ensure that it stayed wherever it landed. *If it landed,* he thought.

He walked down the block and stopped at Mrs. Younger's house. *This is the only place I stopped, the only place I put the bag down.* He looked under the bushes inside Mrs. Younger's fence. It wasn't there.

He looked up her walkway just as Mrs. Younger opened her front door.

"Everything all right, Trevor?" she yelled.

Do I tell her what I'm looking for? He paused. *Can't.* "Yeah," he yelled. "Just looking for something!"

"What?" she yelled back.

"Umm . . . nothing . . . don't worry about it."

"All right. Whatever it is. I hope you find it." And she closed the door.

Marshal was coming as I was leaving. He handed me my backpack. He had a chance to take it. Trevor immediately looked in the driveway for Marshal's car. It was gone.

All right. Calm down. I have a suspect. I have three. But first, I have to finish backtracking before I jump to any conclusions.

So, that's what Trevor did. He turned the corner and traced every step of the way back to school looking everywhere on the ground for the card. He even got the janitor to let him back into the building, so he could check his path back to his desk. Still, it was nowhere.

A lump formed in Trevor's throat, and he felt like he was going to cry. He started to, but stopped himself.

He was mad . . . at himself, for taking the card to school. *I had to, though. It was so cool, and everyone wanted to see it.* He then became scared. Scared of what might happen to him.

As soon as he got out of the school building, he ran home, desperately trying to hold back his tears.

CHAPTER EIGHT
The Pickle

Trevor dreaded going inside. He knew Kirsten would be home from school by now. She got home later than usual because of cheerleading practice. He had to act calm, as if everything were normal.

Act normal. Easier said than done. He was still holding back his tears. He went inside.

Great-grandpa, Kirsten, and his mom were together in the living room talking. He walked through the door and immediately had six eyes glaring at him. He was a little out of breath from running, and his eyes were red. He didn't know what to say.

"Hi, honey." It was his mom. "Where'd you go in such a hurry?"

A pause.

"School . . . I forgot something I needed for class tomorrow." He lied. *I can't believe I just did that.* Now he was as bad as Frank Carbone. He hated lying to his mother—to anyone for that matter. The first time he lied to his mother was when he was eight and he came home with

49

green paint stains on his pants. His mother asked him what it was from. He said he was playing baseball, and it was a new kind of green dirt. The truth was that some older boys had talked him and his friend, Scott, into playing near a water tower. He wasn't allowed to play there. The paint was from a fence he climbed to get there. *I lied then to stay out of trouble, too,* he thought.

His lie was more believable now than at age eight. After all, who ever heard of green baseball dirt? And he didn't like the fact that he sounded so believable.

His mother looked at him strangely because he didn't have a book or anything in his hand. Maybe he wasn't such a good liar after all.

"Uhhh . . . I'm gonna go up to my room for a while," Trevor said waving to Kirsten, his mom and great-grandpa. On his way up the stairs he casually looked again at his great-grandpa who still wasn't making total eye contact with him. But right now that was the least of his problems.

"He's so weird," Kirsten commented. "Are you sure he's related to me?" she said with her teenage attitude.

Trevor's mom didn't question her son's statement, though her motherly instinct told her something was up.

Trevor sat on his bed with his head between his knees. He had no clue where the card could be. *Was it stolen? What if it wasn't stolen? What if I really lost it?* Trevor couldn't take it anymore. He was scared, and he began to cry.

He tried hard to hold back the tears, but they welled up inside him until they flowed like a gusher. He tried to cry quietly. *Dad will be home soon.* This thought did not make Trevor feel any better, although the crying did.

Trevor dried his tears with his shirt sleeve and blew his nose. He hit his pillow as hard as he could, then sat on his bed with his head down and his hands over his eyes.

What do I do?! The thought yelled inside his brain. He didn't have many options. He quickly got up and began pacing around his room.

I could call the cops. I could put up "Lost" signs . . . Then everyone would know, especially mom, dad and great-grandpa—and the kids at school. Kirsten's teasing him for being such a lame brain was hardly a concern now.

He looked again at the backpack. *It couldn't have fallen out.* Which led him back to Marshal Younger, Jim Evans and Tom Murphy. *It could have been stolen. They were the only other people to touch my bag. Do I ask them if they took it? What if they didn't? How would I feel being accused of something like that? Should I tell mom and dad?* A long pause. *No. I've got to solve this myself.*

That left him with one option—investigate. *I'll start with the first person who had my bag—Marshal Younger.*

Trevor slipped back out of his house undetected. He stood outside the Younger house replaying the day's events in his mind. He looked on the ground again to make doubly sure the card wasn't there. Then he looked in the driveway—Marshal's car was there. *What do I say?* This was serious. The only person he'd ever accused before was his sister, and that was for using or taking something that was his.

He wished he wasn't alone, but this was something he had to do by himself. In any other circumstance, if something this important had been taken from him, he'd have his mom or dad with him for support. He brought his mom with him five years earlier to his friend Ginger's when she had broken his pinwheel and wouldn't give it back to him. *I knew Ginger had my pinwheel,* he thought. *I don't know if he has the card.* But he had to find out.

How do I do this? His finger slowly moved to ring the doorbell. It rang. *No turning back now.* Seconds later the door opened. It was Marshal himself.

"Hey guy," Marshal said in a friendly, innocent and welcoming manner. "What can I do for ya? You want my mom?"

"No . . . I, uhhh, want to talk to you." A pause. "I was wondering . . . I lost something earlier today and umm . . . I thought you might have found it. I lost it back there." He pointed to where his backpack was.

"Sorry, little guy. I didn't find anything. What was it? If I find it, I'll let you know."

"Oh nothing . . . don't worry about it. I . . . I gotta go." Trevor turned and walked away.

He sounded like he was telling the truth. But most liars are good at that. If he stole it, why would he give it back? Ugh! I should have just asked him if he took it while I had the chance. Trevor knew inside he couldn't do that. A tear welled up in his eye again, and he quickly wiped it off as it rolled down his cheek.

He was back in his room. He successfully avoided all conversation on his way in. His dad would be home soon. He tried to take matters into his own hands with no success, and there were still two more suspects. But he couldn't accuse them, and he couldn't go after them now. He was scared and he needed help, but who on earth could help him? The only answer was that he had to tell his parents. He was caught in a pickle.

Oh, no.

CHAPTER NINE

First Things Last

"You lost it!" It was his father. He wasn't happy.

"Dad . . . shhhhh . . . I don't want great-grandpa to know . . ."

"Honey . . ." Trevor's mom kicked in, trying to calm her husband.

"He's gonna have to know." Trevor's father's hand flew up in the air.

Trevor's eyes widened with fear. A pause.

"All right, he doesn't have to know right now." He calmed himself down. "Now tell us . . . what happened?"

Trevor told them the whole story—about bringing the card to school, great-grandpa being called a liar, and showing all the kids the card. He went on about the walk home, helping Mrs. Younger, Marshal handing him his backpack, the near fight with Frank Carbone, Jim and Tom handing him his pack, discovering it was gone and backtracking every move he'd made. Then he told them about going back to see Marshal.

"You didn't accuse him, did you, honey?" his mom asked concerned.

"No. I just asked him if he found anything."

"How'd he react?" Trevor's father inquired.

"He acted like he didn't know what I was talking about. He said if he found something he'd let me know."

They were all sitting on the bed in his parent's bedroom; it was tense and quiet. No one really knew what to say–or what to do.

"Trev . . . what do you want me to do? I can't go to the Younger's or Jim and Tom's parents and accuse them of stealing the card. I can't call the Police on them; there's no evidence. You didn't see any of them take it, right?"

"No."

"Then I can't accuse them. Are you sure you didn't lose it?"

A tear ran down Trevor's face. "I don't know. I went back. I traced my steps. I couldn't find it. I'm sorry. I'm sorry." He was sobbing now and in his mother's arms. His mom gently and lovingly stroked his hair. She looked at her husband. Neither were sure exactly what to do.

"Tell you what . . . Your father and I will walk back with you," his mother said. "We'll look, too. Three pairs of eyes should be able to find it if it's still out there. Okay?"

Trevor was sniffling now. He had his tears under control.

"All right," he said, a bit choked up.

"Hey . . . What's all the hubbub about in here?" It was great-grandpa.

Trevor looked at his father.

A pause. "Umm, nothing, grandpa. Everything's all right," Trevor's dad said.

54

Great-grandpa looked at Trevor. Even though he was still hurt, he didn't like seeing his great-grandson upset.

"Anything I can do to help?"

"No . . . we have it covered for now. Thanks, grandpa," Trevor's father said.

Great-grandpa didn't push the matter any further. He knew when to stay out of parenting business. "All right," he said. "If you need me you know where to find me." And he walked away.

"Thanks," Trevor said taking a deep breath. He felt better, but he was emotionally wiped out.

"Hey, this is just for now. We at least need a chance to find it and think some more before we worry him with what happened," Mr. Mitchell said. A pause. "So . . . you ready? Shall we start the hunt?"

"This is important. I think we need one more pair of eyes on this effort." It was Trevor's mom. Trevor looked at her curiously. "I think we should take Kirsten along."

"Oh, mom . . ." Trevor whined. "No. No way. I don't want her to know. She'll never let me live it down."

"Trev. You know how good she is at finding things."

"Yeah, but . . ."

"Your mother's right," Trevor's dad added. "I'll make sure she doesn't tease you. She's old enough to understand how important this is. I agree with your mother though." He started to chuckle. "That kid can find anything."

"But dad . . . I, I don't want the kids at school to find out. If she knows . . ."

"I'll make her promise not to tell anyone," his father overlapped. "She'll keep her word. You can trust her, Trev."

Trevor thought hard for a second. *I can't believe I'm saying this.* "All right." A pause. "But she better not say anything . . . to anyone."

They all walked together–Trevor, his mom, dad, and Kirsten–backtracking Trevor's course home from school and looking at the ground as they walked.

Great-grandpa was still at home. He felt a little left out when they didn't ask him to come for their "walk," but their mission couldn't include him right now.

The Mitchells searched every square inch along the sidewalk. They moved branches, looked behind fire hydrants, in flower beds, anywhere and everywhere the card might have fallen.

"I bet we look pretty silly to the neighbors," Kirsten joked.

Her comment caused everyone to laugh, even Trevor.

They continued looking, following Trevor's path home.

"Trev," his father asked. "How come you did this by yourself before coming to us?"

"I wanted to make sure it was lost . . ."

"And . . ." his father added.

"And I was scared. I didn't want to get in trouble."

"You went and talked to Marshal Younger, too, without your mom and me."

"I know. I'm sorry."

"I'm glad you're sorry. I want you to know you can always come to us when you have a problem, okay? Don't be afraid of us." A pause. "I owe you an apology, too. I was only thinking about the dollar value of the card when I got mad. I didn't think once about how you were feeling. I apologize."

"That's okay, dad. We shouldn't even be having to do this. I broke the rule. I took the card out of the house."

"That's right, you did, and we'll talk about that later. For now, the fact that the card is gone is punishment enough . . . for all of us. I just want you to come to us first next time. All right?" His dad assured.

"You too, Kirsten," Trevor's mom said.

"I will!" she affirmed.

"You know, kids . . . we adults do the same thing sometimes. Sometimes when we have a problem, we go and try to do everything ourselves to solve the problem before we bring it to the Lord. We all need to go to God for help first."

"Believe me, dad . . . I've been praying big time," Trevor exclaimed.

The Mitchell family went to school and back searching every inch of the way. Unfortunately, when they went up the walkway to their front door, they were still empty-handed.

Trevor was sad and wanted to cry again, but mom, dad, and Kirsten reassured him everything would be all right. They prayed together that the Lord would somehow help bring the card back to them.

That night, it was raining hard outside. Under normal circumstances Trevor would have been watching the baseball game on television with great-grandpa, but Trevor didn't want to be near him now. He couldn't face him, not with all that had happened in the past eight hours. Instead, Trevor sat by his bedroom window watching the thunderstorm, thinking if the card were out there, it was surely ruined by now. *Not even the plastic case would protect it from rain like this.*

CHAPTER TEN
Hardball

The bell rang for recess, and all the sixth-graders of Calvin Coolidge elementary school began to take over the playground. Trevor exited the school alone on purpose. He had one thing on his mind now—the investigation. He still had two more suspects.

He had watched enough detective shows on television to know that finding out the right answers meant asking the right questions—of the right people. He had suspects—Jim Evans and Tom Murphy. He had a motive. Now, he just needed to discover if his hunches were true.

Where to start? I can't just come out and ask them. I have to be sneaky. I stink at being sneaky. Why couldn't I have paid more attention to all those detective shows?

Trevor looked around the playground and spotted Jim Evans. *Good. He's alone. Where's Frank?* Trevor perused the kickball game and the basketball court. *There he is, playing basketball.* A pause. *Oh, no. Tom is with him. I'll deal with him later.* Frank scored a basket and started dancing around rubbing his skill into the other kids' faces. Frank was cocky all right. "Lord, help me find this card," Trevor said to himself. He quickly looked for Jim again. He was still alone, but heading for the field. *This may be my only chance.*

"Hey, Jim!" Trevor shouted, running up to him.

Jim turned around and looked at Trevor like "why are you calling me?"

"Hey . . . How's it going?"

"Good," Jim said, looking as if he'd been asked a nuclear physics question. "What do you want?"

"Me? Oh, nothing really . . . I was just wondering . . . ummm . . . you, you collect baseball cards?" Trevor winced, but looked intensely at Jim's face for a reaction. *Oh! too obvious . . . Stupid. Think!*

"Yeah. Of course I do. Who doesn't?" Jim replied. "Why you wanna know, Mitchell?"

"No reason. I, I started collecting cards a while back. I thought maybe you and I could trade. Maybe . . . you can show me your collection sometime." Trevor looked closely at Jim's face to see if he showed any sign of guilt or suspicion.

"I don't think so. Your collection's definitely better than mine," he said, referring to the Babe Ruth card. "I only have new stuff." Jim paused a moment, then the businessman inside him came out. "But . . . I'm always willing to trade some doubles. You have any Yankees?"

Trevor was still looking in Jim's eyes for a sign, any sign, that Jim was the one who had his card.

"Hello . . . are you listening Mitchell?" Jim exclaimed shaking his head.

"Umm. Yeah. Yeah. I've got some Yankees. I even have doubles."

"Cool. Maybe we can do a trade sometime."

"Little help!" It was one of the kids from the kickball game. The ball suddenly came flying over to where Jim and Trevor were standing.

"Come on, Jim! Get in the game!" one of the boys yelled. Jim picked up the red playground ball and threw it back to the other kids.

"Gotta go, Mitchell! Hey, when we trade, can you bring that Ruth card? I'd sure like to see it again!" he shouted running onto the field.

"Uhhh . . . Sure!" Trevor replied, knowing that if he had it, he'd never ever take it out of his house again.

Man. This is hard. Harder than it looks on TV. He looked sincere though. He didn't flinch one bit when I asked to see his collection . . . Maybe he was on to me? Maybe he asked to see the card to try to throw me off? What do I do now?

Trevor quickly turned his head and saw Ginger.

"Hey, Ginger!" *Private Eye Rule Number 101 . . . always look for witnesses.*

"No, I didn't see anything," Ginger answered. "Why?"

"No reason. I just thought that maybe you might have seen something . . . 'illegal' happen during the fight," Trevor replied. "You didn't see anyone take anything . . . from anyone . . . anywhere?"

"No. Why do you ask? And why are you beating around the bush? This is me, remember. You've known me forever. What's up?"

"Nothing. Nothing's up," Trevor said half-convincingly.

"I know you, Trevor Mitchell. I can tell when something's wrong. What is it? Maybe I can help."

"Seriously. Nothing's wrong. I'm . . . I'm all right," Trevor assured her. "Maybe I can tell you later."

61

"Fine. Be that way," Ginger said, her feelings a little bent out of shape. "I thought we were friends."

"We are . . ."

"Have your secrets then. See if I care," she said walking away.

"Ginger! Come on!" Trevor yelled, but she didn't turn around. Trevor shook his head and looked down at the ground. *I'm not doing so well. Man. I need help. I'm gonna bust if I don't tell someone soon. You should've told her . . . She can't keep a secret though.*

Trevor looked up and noticed his friend Whitey playing stickball with two other guys. On any normal day Trevor would be playing, too. Stickball was a great way to practice one's swing for baseball. Trevor watched enviously for a moment, longing to play, but he didn't need to do that right now. *What I need is help. But who can I trust?* He looked over at Whitey. *Whitey can keep a secret. He never told anyone I kissed Jennifer Sanders last marking period. And he knows everybody.*

Trevor then walked over to where the boys were playing stickball, called time out, took Whitey aside and told him everything. Whitey's job was to be Trevor's eyes and ears. He would be "the informer" if he heard anything suspicious.

Whitey really didn't want to help Trevor, which was pretty typical for Whitey. He didn't like to go out of his way for people. He was friends with different cliques of kids only because he was like a chameleon, changing his personality according to whomever he was with. At least my secret is safe with him, Trevor thought.

The stickball game resumed—without Trevor. Trevor turned his attention to the basketball court where Tom Murphy was still shooting hoops.

"Excuse me! Trevor! Trevor Mitchell!"

Oh no. It was Mr. Jenkins, the principal. *What does he want? Doesn't this guy ever work?* "Uhhh . . . yes, sir," Trevor answered.

"I've been looking for you. I have a great idea that I'm sure you're gonna love."

Trevor looked at him curiously.

"Our guest speaker for Friday's Assembly canceled on me this morning. At first I was very upset . . . then I remembered you."

"Me?"

"Yes. I remembered you . . . and your grandfather . . ."

"Great-grandfather," Trevor interjected.

"Oh, yes . . . your great-grandfather. I think it would be wonderful if he would come to the assembly Friday and talk to everyone about playing in the major leagues . . . and about 'The Babe.' I just love that story. He was great on CNN®. So were you."

"Thanks," Trevor said with very little enthusiasm.

"I'm sure everyone would just love it—and it would sure help me out if you know what I mean?" he said softly.

Trevor stood there frozen. *I think that's the worst idea I ever heard in my life.*

"Ummm. I don't know. He's pretty busy," Trevor awkwardly answered.

"Can you ask him?" A pause. Mr. Jenkins saw the look of uneasiness on Trevor's face. "Oh . . . I should probably call your parents and ask myself. That would probably be best now, wouldn't it?"

"I . . . I'm not sure . . ." Trevor stammered. "I . . ."

"Oh! And we'll have to have him bring the card. That would be like . . . awesome," he said, trying to be cool.

"Wouldn't it? I heard you had it here yesterday. I'd really like to see it. Do you have it with you now?

"Uhhh, no. No, I don't. Uhhh . . ."

"That's all right . . . Thanks Trevor. This is great. I'll call your house tonight. This should be a very memorable assembly. Hey now . . . the bell should be ringing soon. Study hard. Study, study, study, I always say. We'll see you later."

"Yeah . . . bye," Trevor said softly as Mr. Jenkins walked away.

Memorable? You're not kidding. What a week I'm having! No one believes him. They'll laugh at him. I can't let that happen. All this . . . because of that stupid card.

CHAPTER ELEVEN
Cut-off Play

"You can't let him speak to the class. They'll laugh at him. Please, when Mr. Jenkins calls you, don't answer, or say he's not here, that he went away; say anything, but don't let great-grandpa speak at that assembly," Trevor pleaded with his mother.

"Honey . . . I can't lie to Mr. Jenkins. Grandpa didn't go away. He's here," his mother gently said.

"Just don't give great-grandpa the call. He'll say yes. He doesn't know about the card. He . . ."

"He's still pretty hurt, Trev. He may not even want to do it. Even if he's asked."

There was a long pause. Trevor looked down at the floor. He didn't know what to do or say anymore.

"You two still haven't made up. You've never gone this long not talking to him. You can't avoid him forever, you know."

"But mom . . . I just don't know what to do . . . what to think."

"What do you think?" his mother asked.

"I just told you. I don't know." Trevor took a deep breath. He put his elbows on the kitchen table and cupped his chin in his hands.

"Life is never simple, is it Trev?"

"Tell me about it," Trevor replied.

"Trev, let me tell you something about people . . . and life, for that matter. People are sometimes the hardest things to understand. I'll admit that when I first heard your great-grandpa's story, I thought that maybe he had an overactive imagination. Especially when he got to the part about hearing God say, 'Run.' For a while, I wondered if maybe he felt guilty for humbling Babe Ruth that day, so he needed to shift credit to a higher power. But, then, as I got to know him better, I knew that he was a man of his word who had no reason to lie. Most men would brag about it and say it was all their own doing–that they were so great. Your great-grandpa says it was by the grace of God. Sometimes with people . . . and with life, we just have to take things on faith. I believe grandpa's story."

"You do?"

"Yes, I do. It's all right to question things; that's how we learn and grow. That's how we discover truth. Just don't let your mind or heart be ruled by doubt. You have to choose what you are going to believe and what you're not, but there are some things that you just have to take on faith. You understand?"

Trevor didn't answer right away. He was still processing his mother's words. Then he smiled. "Yeah," he said feeling better. "I do."

"Blessed are they that believe who have not seen, right?"

"That's right," he said, grasping the connection. "But

what about great-grandpa? I hurt his feelings . . . and Principal Jenkins is gonna call about the assembly. And the card is gone. This is a mess . . ."

"What do you think you should do?" she asked.

Trevor approached his great-grandfather timidly. He hated the way he was feeling.

Great-grandpa was sitting in his chair channel surfing. He saw Trevor out of the corner of his eye, but didn't acknowledge him. As old and wise as he was, he was still human and a bit stubborn. His word had been questioned by one of his "favorite" people. In a way, Trevor called him a liar, and being called a liar at any age by anyone is never a good thing.

"Great-grandpa . . ." Trevor said. *He must hate me.* "Great-grandpa . . ."

Jack Mitchell turned and acknowledged Trevor's presence.

"Hello, Trevor," he said. There was no usual smile or hug.

"Great-grandpa . . . I want you to know . . . I'm, I'm sorry for what I said the other day."

"You're sorry I heard you," he honestly said back.

A pause. "No . . ." Trevor replied. "I'm sorry for what I said . . . and for what I was thinking. I didn't mean to doubt you. I just did. I don't know what came over me. I'm really sorry. I didn't want to hurt your feelings . . ." Trevor didn't know what else to say.

His great-grandfather turned the TV off and looked at Trevor. He could tell the little boy standing before him was sincere in his apology. He also understood how some might think his story was "out there." He also knew that when someone says "I'm sorry," the next step must be forgiveness.

"Come here, Trev . . . apology accepted." He opened his arms and slowly embraced his great-grandson. His arms were shaking a bit, and it took a second for him to pull Trevor in close.

"I love you, great-grandpa,"

"I love you, too, Trev. You're the apple of my eye, you know that?"

Trevor smiled looking into his great-grandpa's eyes. He looked relieved.

His mother watched the whole thing through the living room door. She smiled, clasping her hands, and winked at her son. There is something very special about hearts and lives being reconciled, she thought. It's the kind of thing that causes angels to rejoice in heaven.

Trevor removed himself from the embrace.

"There's something else I want you to know, okay? I believe you, great-grandpa . . . I really do."

"That's okay, Trev. I imagine Daniel's great-grandson had a hard time believing his great-grandpa survived the den of lions. I understand."

Trevor's great-grandfather held up his hand for a high five, and Trevor hit it. "Watch the ball game together tonight?" he asked. "Hasn't been the same without you."

"Yeah, definitely!" Trevor replied.

"Maybe we can even have a catch later?" great-grandpa said. "We can work on that fielding of yours. You're good, but if you wanna make it to the big leagues you gotta practice. Yeah . . . I think a catch is just what we need. I've missed that with you, too."

"Great-grandpa . . ." Trevor said with a huge smile. "I hope I have half your energy when I'm your age."

"You have half now, sport," Jack Mitchell replied with a wink and a chuckle.

Trevor glanced through the door at his mom who was smiling at him. He smiled back. But there was still more that Trevor had on his mind.

"Ummm, great-grandpa?" Trevor said timidly.

"Yes?"

"There's something else I need to tell you . . ." Trevor looked again at his mom whose eyes replied, 'Go ahead.' "Uhh . . . it's about the Babe Ruth card . . ." Trevor hesitated and looked away.

"Yes, Trevor. What is it?"

"Please don't get mad . . . but . . . I . . . I . . . have something terrible to tell you." He had his great-grandpa's complete attention.

"I, I . . . umm . . . I, I . . . lost the card. I didn't mean to do it," he said quickly. "But it's gone. I'm sorry. I may have lost it . . . or it might have been stolen by some kids at school," he quickly blurted out. "I should've never taken it out of the house. I'm sorry. Please don't get mad."

Great-grandpa paused for a long moment. To Trevor it seemed like forever.

"It's all right, Trev," he said reassuringly. "I'm not mad. It was just a piece of paper with a man's image on it," he added.

"It was worth fifty thousand dollars," Trevor commented.

"Anyone who'd spend fifty thousand dollars on a baseball card when there's so many starving and needy people in the world is a jerk."

Trevor looked at him, surprised that he said jerk.

"Well . . . it's true," he stated. "Now, don't you worry about it, okay? I'm not mad. It'll turn up."

Trevor's mouth opened wide. This was not the reaction he expected. *I guess I don't know him that well after all.* "Yeah. Thanks. I'm sorry. You don't know what I've been through lately."

"I could imagine," great-grandpa said. There was a special light in his eyes, a light that revealed a warm, loving, compassionate heart. Trevor saw in those eyes something he'd known all his life—love and friendship. "Trev, you know why I'm not mad?"

"No." Trevor answered. "But believe me I'm glad."

"Remember when I gave you the card on my birthday?"

"Of course."

"Remember what I told you?"

Jack Mitchell reminded Trevor about the true meaning of the card. The card was special not because of the man on it, but because it reminded him of how God intervened in his life in a miraculous way. The Lord revealed himself to Jack Mitchell in many ways since that time, but always through His Word and by His Spirit.

The day he stole home off of Babe Ruth marked the beginning of Trevor's great-grandfather's spiritual journey.

Babe Ruth was a great baseball player, but on and off the field, well . . . let's just say that he dabbled in many of the sinful pleasures the world has to offer. If anyone needed the Lord's grace, it was certainly "The Babe." He was a man blessed by God with great talent, but only once did Trevor's great-grandfather hear Babe Ruth give credit to the Lord for anything and that was after his so-called "Called Shot"—a homerun that he called and hit after he pointed to the center field bleachers with his bat. After he hit it he said, "the Good Lord must've been with me that day." That was the only expression of gratitude to the Giver of All Good Things that great-grandpa ever heard from George Herman Ruth.

"You understand its meaning, right son?" great-grandpa asked. "Yeah, I understand," Trevor said.

"Good. Then with or without the card, always remember the story. Baseball is a great game with great men, but it is, after all, just a game. I believe you know and love the Lord with all your heart, and you will use your gifts to glorify Him in whatever you do. You just think about God's faithfulness. He is so faithful."

"You bet, great-grandpa. I will," Trevor promised, kissing his favorite Old-Timer.

Trevor then told great-grandpa his whole story. He included how he had one more suspect to investigate—and how the principal was going to call soon with a special invitation. He told him how the kids at school didn't believe the story—and even more important, that the principal was going to ask him to bring the Babe Ruth card to the assembly . . . if he went.

"Well," Jack Mitchell said. "We'll just have to do something about that!"

"But what?" Trevor asked.

"I don't know. But we'll pray for wisdom."

"In all things God works for the good of those who love him," Trevor replied. It was a Scripture verse he memorized three weeks ago for Sunday School. It sure came in handy now.

"That's right," great-grandpa said smiling. "That's right."

CHAPTER TWELVE
Old Timer's Day

The Calvin Coolidge elementary school gym was filled with fourth- through sixth-graders. And for children with varying degrees of attention spans, they were well-behaved as Jack Mitchell talked. He was wearing his old, woolen Detroit Tigers jersey, which looked older than he did, and a Tigers cap. The cap was new—a present from Trevor's father last Christmas.

Jack had two things in his favor on this day. First, most of the kids had never seen a 100-year-old man before. Second, it was only some of the kids in Trevor's sixth grade class who didn't believe the story. The rest either didn't have an opinion or didn't really care.

Trevor sat strategically in the front row, off to the left, where he could view certain people. It was hard for him to sit still. A secret operation was underway. He was excited, worried and anxious all at the same time. *I hope this plan works.*

Mr. Jenkins and all the teachers sat off to the side. Everyone was focused on great-grandpa as he told the story they were all familiar with.

73

"You should have seen the look on Babe Ruth's face," he concluded. "He looked like I had stolen the cup right out of his jockstrap."

The crowd laughed, especially Mr. Jenkins.

"And never before and never since had anyone stolen home off of Babe Ruth. God was surely with me that day."

"What a crock." It was said softly, but loud enough for everyone, even great-grandpa to hear. The comment caused some kids to laugh. Mr. Jenkins looked intensely into the crowd to see who said it, and to give an unspoken message not to say anything again. Trevor looked down, though. He recognized the voice.

Jack Mitchell was unfazed. "Now . . . your principal, Mr. Jenkins, asked me if I would bring the Babe Ruth card to show you guys . . . I know many of you haven't seen many things that old. Heck, I'm probably the oldest thing you've ever seen."

The kids and teachers laughed some more.

"I've got one foot in the grave and another on a banana peel." It was a line everyone in Trevor's family had heard for years, at least since great-grandpa turned 80.

Great-grandpa then looked at Trevor and nodded. Operation Curveball, as they called it, was about to take place. "Where was I . . . oh yeah . . . the card. How many of you are interested in seeing it?"

Almost everyone raised their hand. "All righty then . . . well . . ."

Here we go. Trevor quickly looked into the audience and spotted his target. There were other people he'd like to watch, but only one person mattered right now.

"Well, here it is." With that said, great-grandpa reached into the pocket of his navy blue slacks and pulled out a

Babe Ruth rookie card in a plastic holder. Trevor's eyes were locked on Tom Murphy.

Gasps and words like "cool" and "neat" were heard from the crowd, mostly from boys and girls who loved collecting sports cards; others were from kids who just liked seeing something so old. But Tom Murphy's reaction was . . . *nothing. Not even a blink. No double take? No look of shock? I don't believe it?!*

Trevor's eyes grew wide and his mouth dropped open. Operation Curveball didn't work. Tom Murphy looked at the card just like everyone else. *I guess he didn't take it. But who then?* Trevor quickly looked at his great-grandpa—what do we do now? Great-grandpa understood from Trevor's eyes that the plan didn't work. He turned his attention back to the assembly.

"I want you to know that this card, even though it may be old and worth a lot of money, isn't as important as everyone thinks it is," great-grandpa said.

Fact is, the card he held in his hand wasn't old at all. Trevor and great-grandpa went to Charlie's Sports Collectibles and told him what had happened. They wanted to see if anyone had tried to sell a 1915 Babe Ruth rookie card. No one had, but then it occurred to great-grandpa that they needed something to show the kids at the assembly so no one would know that Trevor didn't have the card anymore, and Operation Curveball was subsequently born. The card in his hand was a reprint that Charlie ordered and had overnighted to the Mitchell family. The shipping cost more than the two-dollar card.

"What's important is that you all know that anything can happen in life . . ." A long pause. Great-grandpa looked at Mr. Jenkins for a cue. Mr. Jenkins motioned for him to go on.

"Ummm . . . then . . . all right. Does anyone have any questions?"

He looked out over the crowd. So did Trevor.

"I do!" a voice proclaimed.

"What's your name son?' great-grandpa asked.

"Frank Carbone."

Trevor looked down and shook his head. *Oh great.*

"How do you explain that there are no records of the game when you stole home?"

"I see you've read the article," great-grandpa said. "Well, Frank . . . to be honest . . . I can't explain it. God only knows. I don't know what happened. I take it you don't believe me?"

Frank was on the spot. He never expected he'd be challenged, and he didn't want to be rude, but he was still Frank Carbone—and Frank Carbone doesn't back down. "Ummm. Well, to be honest . . . ummm . . . No, I don't believe it. Babe Ruth was the greatest. If there were records to prove it . . ."

Jack Mitchell smiled at Frank. "Frank, you obviously know your baseball. Babe Ruth was great, but he was only a man, really no different than you or me. You're a bright young man and not the first person to bring up the records question. All I can say is that it happened. There can't be records of all our accomplishments." A pause. An inspiration. "Which leads me to what I really wanted to share with you people today . . . You know our accomplishments, like stealing home off Babe Ruth . . . or our things, our possessions, like this card . . . don't really matter at all."

The kids all looked at him curiously. They had been taught the total opposite for years. Even Mr. Jenkins and the teachers looked at great-grandpa funny now.

"What matters is . . . well, look around you. Go ahead, look around."

Everyone looked to their left and right not sure of exactly what they were supposed to be looking at.

"What you see here . . . your friends, your teachers, your parents . . . that is what really matters. Believe me . . . it all goes by so fast. *It seems like only yesterday I was your age.* And when you're old like me, you'll think back to Coolidge school and remember your friends who you studied with, played with, dreamed with. I want you to think about it this way, and this is the last thing I'm going to say. There are only two things that matter in life: God and people . . . because they are the only two things that can last forever. Don't ever forget that, and you will have a rich, full life."

There was complete silence until a few of the teachers realized that he really wasn't going to say anything more. They started to clap, and soon the whole assembly was clapping. *I want to be just like you, great-grandpa.* Trevor was proud of his great-grandpa. The fact that Operation Curveball flopped didn't matter anymore. Hearing words spoken from a man like great-grandpa made quite an impression on anyone on the receiving end. This was an assembly that no one would forget. Mr. Jenkins got up and shook great-grandpa's hand and escorted him off the stage.

"Hey, Mitchell!" It was Tom Murphy with Frank Carbone.

The assembly had been over for over an hour. The bell had rung. Trevor and everyone else were leaving their classes to go home.

Oh boy. What do they want? A pause. "Hey . . . listen I don't want to hear anymore 'bout this lying stuff, okay . . ." Trevor started.

"Hey . . . we weren't going to," Tom said. A pause. He looked at Frank. "Actually . . . actually . . . I think your great-grandpa's pretty cool," Tom said.

"You do?" Trevor was shocked.

"Yeah, and I was wondering if maybe you could get me his autograph . . . on a baseball?"

Frank looked at Tom like he was crazy.

Trevor was taken aback. He then thought he'd investigate some more though, just to be sure. "How'd you guys like that card?" Trevor asked.

"It's cool," Tom said. "I wish my grandfather or my father kept something like that from when they were kids."

Huh? They have no idea.

"So . . . about the ball, could you?" Tom asked.

"You want one, too?" Trevor asked Frank.

Frank paused. An autographed baseball is always a cool thing to have. "No, that's all right, Mitchell. I still don't think it ever happened," Frank replied.

"Well, that's your choice, Frank. Maybe someday you'll have faith that it actually happened."

"Nice try, Mitchell. I don't think so."

Trevor turned his attention to Tom. "Tell you what, you supply the ball, and I'll get you the autograph."

"Thanks," Tom replied.

Trevor looked at Frank who obviously felt awkward. Trevor stuck out his hand. "Listen, Frank, just because you don't believe my great-grandpa doesn't mean we can't be friends. What do ya say? . . ."

Frank looked at Trevor's hand. Tom looked at Frank as if to say, "shake it." "Well . . . I heard my dad say he's gonna try and draft you for our team next year, so . . . since we may be on the same team . . . I guess it's all right." He shook his hand quickly. Frank wasn't used to making up.

Trevor stood there speechless.

"We'll see ya later," said Tom as he and Frank walked away.

"Yeah . . . I'll see you later," Trevor exclaimed. And the boys walked down the hall. Trevor then noticed Ginger walking out of her classroom. He waved and smiled at her. She smiled in return. *Good. She's not mad at me anymore.*

The card was still gone, but things were looking up for Trevor. He felt some sort of order returning to his life, and his posture and the way he walked reflected it.

Coming down the hallway toward him was Whitey. He was alone. He casually bent down to get a drink from the water fountain as Trevor approached him. Then, suddenly, he jolted erect as a stream of water launched toward the sky. His face was dripping wet. It seems somebody jammed a piece of popsicle stick in the fountain, causing it to act like a high-pressure squirt gun.

"A little thirsty, Whitey?" Trevor said, laughing. "The water's supposed to go inside your mouth." It was the first joke from Trevor in days.

"Very funny," Whitey replied. "Did you do that?" he said, referring to the popsicle stick.

"No, you probably did it and forgot it was there," Trevor jokingly replied again.

"What are you so happy about?"

"Oh, nothing. I'm just feeling good. God is good to me . . . Hey . . . how'd you like the assembly?"

"It was cool. Your great-grandpa's really old, man, so old he probably graduated with George Washington . . ."

"Very funny," Trevor replied, sarcastically.

"You're lucky Carbone didn't give him a harder time."

"I gotta tell you something 'bout that card," Trevor said.

"Yeah . . . I must've missed something in the article. I didn't know he had two cards . . ."

Trevor froze. "What do you mean?" he said with extreme curiosity.

"You have two cards," Whitey said matter-of-factly.

"What makes you think I have two?"

"Huh?" Whitey grunted, not understanding the questioning at all. "What do you mean?"

The look on Trevor's face then got very serious, and Whitey realized something wasn't right.

"How do you know I didn't find mine? What makes you think there are two cards?"

"What are you talking about?" Whitey asked straight-forwardly.

"Nobody knows there are two cards. Why do you think there are two?" Trevor said very seriously.

"Well . . . uhh . . ." Whitey fumbled for an answer.

Trevor's countenance suddenly changed. His thoughts were racing and so was his pulse. He snapped inside.

"It was you, wasn't it? You took my card! I can't believe you!"

"What are you talking about, Mitchell? I didn't take your stupid card," Whitey said. He started to walk away.

"Then how do you know there are two cards then? Nobody knows that except my family . . ."

"I didn't take your stupid card, man! It was probably Murphy or someone else that was at your stupid fight. I wasn't there, remember?" Whitey said trying to avoid Trevor, as Trevor blocked his path with his body.

"Then how do you know? Tell me!" Trevor was more serious now than he'd ever been in his whole life. He was in Whitey's face, practically in Whitey's shoes.

Whitey gave no response. Other kids began to notice and slowed down as they walked by. Some even stopped and watched.

"That card is worth a lot of money. It means a lot to my family! Whoever stole it could be arrested. I want the truth, Scott," Trevor exclaimed, calling him by his real name. "Did you take it?! Tell me." There was a lump in Trevor's throat that felt like an apple. He started to shake.

Whitey looked at the kids who were staring at him. He then turned to Trevor. "No! I didn't take your card! Now get out of my face! You're such a loser, Mitchell! No wonder nobody likes you!" Whitey pushed Trevor aside and walked away.

His last statement was a lie. The other kids did like Trevor. They had no idea what was going on, but they knew it was serious. Ginger overheard most of what just transpired.

"What's going on?" she asked.

"It's a long story," Trevor replied.

"Is this what you couldn't tell me about?"

"Yep," Trevor answered, and he just watched Whitey walking abruptly down the hall. Trevor had no idea what to do now.

CHAPTER THIRTEEN
The Unexpected

The weekend came, and things didn't get back to normal for the Mitchell family. The phone was still ringing off the hook with people calling about the article. It was appearing in more papers across the country. They received some crank calls from Babe Ruth fans who said great-grandpa was a "nut." Other calls came saying great-grandpa was a liar. *The Tonight Show* and *The Rosie O'Donnell Show* called, too.

The family talked it over and decided it would be best if great-grandpa didn't appear anymore on TV. They trusted Jay and Rosie, but they wanted the craziness to end.

CNN® was still broadcasting the segment as well. It was a terrific story and mostly everyone loved it. They also loved Trevor's great-grandpa.

A couple of "crazies," as great-grandpa called them, called with offers to buy the card. Trevor's father simply told them the card was not for sale.

Trevor could not get Whitey out of his mind. He replayed their conversation over and over in his mind. He told his parents and great-grandpa about it, but they couldn't call Whitey's parents and accuse him. It just wouldn't be right. They all did the only thing that mattered most—pray.

Then, on Sunday afternoon, right after church, a telegram arrived at the Mitchell home. It was addressed to Jack Mitchell from a man named Tom McCullough who lived in Florida. Trevor's great-grandpa had never heard of him. Tom McCullough was 108 years old. The telegram read: "Saw your story on CNN®. Glad to know you're still alive. Happy Birthday from someone eight years your senior—who was at the game. You certainly showed up Babe Ruth that day. I can still see your slide. It seems like yesterday! Best regards, Tom McCullough."

Tom McCullough had often wondered what happened to the young rookie who stole home that day. The rookie showed promise. He didn't know that Jack Mitchell only played two years in the majors for Detroit and had to stop playing because of a bad knee.

Trevor's great-grandfather read the telegram and immediately had to sit down. His eyes became misty, and a big tear rolled down his wrinkled cheek. After all these years, here was his proof, but more than that, it just felt good to be remembered.

108 years old. Well, I'll be. Thank you, Tom. Thank you.

"What, grandpa? Who's it from?" Trevor's mom asked.

Everyone was around him. He passed it to Trevor's mom first. She read it and got teary-eyed, too. She passed it to her husband who passed it to Kirsten who passed it to Trevor. Everyone was moved. Trevor finished reading the last line and looked up at everyone with a big smile. They all embraced. It was the family's finest moment.

Later that evening, Trevor's great-grandpa called information and got the number for Tom McCullough in Cocoa Beach, Florida. He called him, and the two spoke for nearly an hour. You'd have thought they were old friends. The main topic of conversation–baseball. Baseball has a special way of bridging communication gaps–even among people who've only just met.

No sooner had Trevor's great-grandpa hung up the phone, when it rang again. It was another surprise. Trevor's mom answered the call. The news she heard was both good and bad.

The woman on the other end of the line was Mrs. Whiteman, Whitey's mom. It seems about an hour ago Whitey told her that he had stolen the card. He felt terrible. He was still crying in his room. She felt terrible, too. Trevor's mom was thrilled and relieved to know that the card was found, but saddened that Whitey had really stolen it.

"Thank you, Mrs. Whiteman. We're very pleased to know where it is. Do you want us to pick it up?" A long pause. "Are you sure you wanna do it that way?" Another pause. "All right . . . no . . . it's all right. Yes . . . I'll talk to you soon." And she hung up.

She took a deep breath. "John! grandpa! kids! . . . come here for a minute, please!" she yelled to the next room.

She then told everyone that Whitey had the card. It seems that Whitey was walking behind Trevor on the way home from school that day. He saw Trevor doing his good deed with Mrs. Younger, and he saw the backpack. He knew the card was in there, and he took it when no one was looking.

Trevor was relieved to know that they were going to have the card back, but he felt angry and betrayed. He had hoped that it wasn't true.

"How are we gonna get it back?" Kirsten asked.

"I'm a little shocked. Mrs. Whiteman is insisting that Scott give it back to Trevor at school tomorrow."

Trevor's eyes grew bigger. "What! I don't even want to see him! Doesn't he know what he put me through?" *Good thing I didn't actually accuse any of those other guys of taking it.* Trevor felt terrible now for even thinking that.

"That's how she wants to do it," his mom stated.

"Think how Whitey is feeling right now," his father said, "knowing he's got to face you." A pause. "The good news is we're getting the card back, right grandpa?"

"God is faithful, and he answers prayer," Trevor's great-grandpa said with a smile. "But that poor little boy."

"We'll pray for him now, too," Kirsten exclaimed.

CHAPTER FOURTEEN
Duty

Trevor's walk to school this time was long and hard. He was excited to get his card back, but he did not want to see Whitey.

I can't believe he did this to me. He was my friend. Trevor couldn't understand what would make Whitey steal from him. He was always nice to Whitey. He helped him with his homework, and when other kids wouldn't talk to him or hang out with him, Trevor always would. That's what a friend was to Trevor, someone who was always there–and who would never steal.

He's no friend of mine, and he NEVER will be again, Trevor thought, approaching the school grounds. *I'm just gonna take the card back and walk away.* Trevor thought about punching him . . . he was certainly mad enough, but he knew that wouldn't solve anything.

He walked onto school property, passed the swing set and there he was. Whitey was standing against the wall by the door to their wing. He was looking about as happy as

Trevor was. Actually, he was looking worse. He was scared, and he knew what he did was terribly wrong.

Trevor walked up to him quickly. *Let's get this over with.*

The two looked at each other awkwardly, not sure who should speak first.

"Can I have my card back . . . please?" Trevor took control.

"Yeah." Whitey reached into his backpack and handed it to him.

Trevor checked it thoroughly to make sure it was not harmed. It looked good.

Trevor didn't say a word. He just looked at Whitey, shook his head, then began to walk for the door. The bell was about to ring, and kids were starting to gather and walk by.

"Wait!" It was Whitey.

Trevor turned around.

"What?" He looked Whitey in the eye.

"I want you to know . . . I'm sorry."

Trevor paused for a moment.

"Sorry? I don't believe you, Whiteman."

"No, Trev. I'm sorry I took it."

"Why'd you do it?" Trevor asked, really wanting to know.

"I don't know why. I saw the backpack sitting there, and something inside said, 'Take it.' I knew it was wrong, but I couldn't help myself. I've felt terrible ever since. I didn't know how to get it back to you."

"How long were you gonna wait?"

"I don't know. I didn't know what to do. I don't have any good answers. I'm sorry."

Trevor looked into Whitey's eyes, into his soul. He

looked sincere. He thought about asking Whitey if he knew how much trouble he caused or if his mother had grounded him for life, but then he thought of how he asked his great-grandpa and his parents to forgive him when he was sorry. They didn't bombard him with questions . . .

"Apology accepted."

Whitey smiled with relief.

Forgiving isn't easy sometimes, but Trevor knew he had to. It was his duty. He would have forgiven Whitey in his own heart later anyway, after he had time to process everything. He knew that.

"Thanks," Whitey said breathing a sigh of relief.

"No problem," Trevor said. "It took a lot of guts to do what you just did."

"It wasn't easy."

"Not many things are, I'm learning. Not many things are." They smiled.

Trevor held the card tightly in his hand. There was no way he was going to put Babe Ruth back in his knapsack. He would call his mom to come get it from him. *That's what I'll do.* He then wondered if he and Whitey would ever be friends again. They would.

Trevor opened the door for Whitey, and they went to school. Lessons, it seemed, weren't always learned from text books. And the lesson Trevor learned during the past few weeks–about faith, family, friendship and forgiveness– were lessons that he'd take with him and use everyday from that time forward.

CHAPTER FIFTEEN
The Weaving

Trevor's great-grandpa passed away five years later. Trevor was 16. His great-grandpa was 105. The card was kept in a secret place in the Mitchell home—only Trevor and his family knew where. And they looked at it often and remembered.

There were tears, of course, when Trevor's great-grandpa died. Lots of them. And as sad as everyone was, no one looked at death as if it were the end because they knew great-grandpa was now safe at home in heaven. And everyone knows there is baseball in heaven.

As he grew into manhood, Trevor became a man of character like his great-grandpa—and he treasured his memories.

With a little faith all things are possible, Trevor thought, remembering his great-grandpa as he brushed the dirt off his pants. He was standing on third base in Tiger Stadium, looking at the best pitcher in the major Leagues—a rookie just like himself. He brushed the dirt off his hands and thought about how much he loved and missed his great-grandpa, and how he knew he was watching from above. Trevor Christian Mitchell then took his lead and looked at the pitcher beginning his wind up. *This one's for you great-grandpa. I love you.* He focused his eyes on home and ran.

WRAP-UP

Fact vs. Fiction

They say that "truth is sometimes stranger than fiction." And although I wouldn't consider any of the fictional elements in *Safe at Home* strange, the story does contain many truthful facts. Here's an overview of the "fact vs. fiction" elements in *Safe at Home*—so you may know what is real and what is a product of my imagination—and so you may be set free!

FACT

Babe Ruth's rookie card really is the 1915 *Sporting News* No. 151 card.

FICTION

The card is not yet quite worth $50,000. Presently, the card books in mint condition for around $3,000.

FACT

Babe Ruth's rookie season was in 1914, when he began his career as a left-handed pitcher for the Boston Red Sox. Babe Ruth pitched 29 2/3 consecutive scoreless innings of

93

World Series' play. He really did say, "the good Lord must have been with me that day," when he referred to his alleged "called shot" home run.

Mike McNally did play third base for the Boston Red Sox in 1915.

Christy Mathewson was nicknamed "The Christian Gentleman." Christy also promised his mom he would not pitch on Sunday.

FICTION

Jack Mitchell is a fictional character I created. I guess you could say he is my dream of what a really cool grandpa or great-grandpa would be like. Therefore, Trevor Mitchell and all the other characters are fictional as well. Trevor was named after my son.

The reference that there are 4 games in baseball history from 1911 to 1932 that no one, not even the Hall of Fame, has records of is fiction.

FACT

There were at least two steals of home while Babe Ruth was pitching. One was on May 16, 1916, when Ruth beat the Browns, 3-1. The only St. Louis score was on a double steal. The second was June 1, 1917, when Ruth lost to Cleveland, 3-0. One of the Indian tallies came on a double steal. Source: *The Baseball Chronology,* by James Charlton, published by Macmillan in 1990

Rob Skead